MAZZY
and the
MONARCHS

by *Diane Lebo* and *Lynn Herklotz*

Diane Lebo

Ronna Lebo

Lynn Herklotz

Mazzy and the Monarchs

story by **Diane Lebo**
and **Lynn Herklotz**

illustrations by
Ronna Lebo

The wind had changed. It was definitely blowing from the North. The leaves had turned brilliant reds, oranges and yellows. Mazzy decided it was a good day for her, for Max and for their cousins, Aidan and Carter to explore the near-by fencerows for milkweed pods.

Gathering Max and two paper bags that had once held groceries, Mazzy started down the drive and across the fence to Aunt El's where the cousins were staying. Aunt El is sister to their Grammy, and Aidan and Carter stay with her when their parents are at work.

"Hello, Auntie El. We want Aidan and Carter to come with us. It's a good day to hunt for milkweed pods." said Mazzy in her usual confident manner.

"The wind is blowing and the beautiful, white, fluffy seeds need to be set free."

She was talking about the milkweed seeds and their white feathery tails.

Asclepias Syriaco

Mazzy had a marvelous imagination and the first time she saw the open milkweed pods release seeds into the wind, she was intrigued by the way they flew; the fluffy feathery seed-tails catching the breeze to soar high across the meadow.

They reminded her of tiny parachutes

"I'm so sorry, Mazzy. Carter is not feeling well. He has a sore throat," said Auntie, "but Aidan is in his room reading. I'm sure he would love to go on an adventure with you and Max."

"Aidan, I really feel like hunting for milkweed pods," Mazzy exclaimed as she pushed open the door to his room, "but Aunt El said Carter is sick, so I guess he won't want to go. Do you?"

Max was concerned. He was not sure what milkweed pods might be, and they sounded a bit like something from a science fiction story or maybe a recipe.

Max is only three-and-a-half.

"That's great," said Aidan, "I have a book about milkweed pods."

(Aidan reads all of the time.)

"Did you know that milkweed nectar is the only food Monarch butterfly larva will eat, and it's the only plant the Monarch butterflies will lay their eggs on?"

Danaus Plerippus

Max relaxed a little. He liked butterflies, so he figured hunting for the seed pods wouldn't be too scary. He was sad though, that Carter was not well. He turned and ran back to the kitchen to tell Auntie El.

"Carter is too sick?" he asked his aunt. "Will he be better for my birthday?"

Max had recently realized that birthdays were very special.

"Oh, I'm sure of it." Aunt El replied, "We will give him an elixir for his sore throat and a bit of lozenge for his cough, and he will be fine by tomorrow or the next day."

Auntie El was famous in the neighborhood for her medicinals, and often one or another neighbor would stop in for a soothing tea or a mixture to warm the throat. Aunt El's herb garden was extensive and she grew many plants that were for healing.

She also grew cooking herbs, like basil and rosemary.

For some reason, the rabbits and deer never bothered Aunt El's garden. She had a salt lick out back for the deer, and grew lettuce and carrots for the rabbits in a separate garden closer to the woods. Somehow, they knew to be content with their own wild gardens and to leave her special garden alone.

Mazzy, Max and Aidan ran happily out of the house towards the fencerows where the milkweed grew.

"There's some, there's some!" rang out over the backyards as the children grabbed, pulled, and plucked the greenish pods and slit them open with a fingernail.

"Watch the parachutes fly!" yelled Mazzy as she turned one of her carefully collected pods inside out and blew on the fluffy seeds in her hand.

Milkweed 'parachutes' flew in all directions as the children twirled into a milkweed seed-flinging dance.

Later, Mother would find milkweed fluff and seeds in both Mazzy and Max's hair and clothes.

Aidan was examining his pods and putting them in his pockets. Aidan always had pockets. He said they were necessary.

"C'mon, Aidan," Mazzy said, flopping on the ground to rest.
"Open the seed pods!"

"I'm going to take them home to plant them," he responded. "I want to grow a milkweed home for the butterflies!"

Max liked this idea. He had picked milkweed pods and blown the down all over himself. His hands and some parts of his face were sticky with milkweed 'milk', and he thought that taking some pods home for the butterflies was a great idea.

"I want a butterfly garden, too," he said. "Will you help me?"

"Sure!" said the others, all at the same time.

"Everybody get some to take home," Mazzy commanded, seeing another project in her future. "Auntie El will help us, too."

The children, pockets, hands and paper bags full of milkweed pods, scampered back up the hill to the house.

"Look, Carter!" Aidan said, running through Auntie El's open back door.

"I brought you some milkweed pods. We'll have a butterfly garden in the springtime!"

This seems to be the end of this adventure, but could be the beginning of yet another!

Danaus Plerippus

Mazzy and the Monarchs was
written by two sisters,
Diane Lebo and Lynn Herklotz

They have also written an earlier
story about the cousins, called
***Mazzy and the Sundrunk
Woodchuck***

The illustrations for both stories
were drawn by Ronna Lebo

(for information about these books,
please write to
rrlebo@mac.com)

OcularPress